Disney
THE MUPPETS
Read-Along
STORYBOOK AND CD

THE MUPPETS have to stage a comeback show to save their theater! To find out what happens, read along with me in your book. You will know it's time to turn the page when you hear this sound. . . .

It's time to meet the Muppets!

LET'S BEGIN NOW.

10 9 8 7 6 5 4 3 2 1

ISBN 978-1-4231-3337-7

V381-8386-5-12034

Visit www.disneybooks.com

SUSTAINABLE FORESTRY INITIATIVE
Certified Chain of Custody
35% Certified Forest Content,
65% Certified Sourcing
www.sfiprogram.org
SFI-00993

Disney PRESS
NEW YORK

WALTER *and* GARY were brothers who did everything together. They were roommates, and they lived in Smalltown, USA. Walter had never really felt at home in Smalltown, but he tried to focus on the fun times he had with Gary. They both loved riding bikes, singing and dancing, and the Muppets . . . they really loved the Muppets. In fact, it was Walter's dream to visit the Muppet Studios in Los Angeles.

GARY *and his* GIRLFRIEND, MARY, were planning to take a trip to Hollywood to celebrate their tenth anniversary. And since the Muppet Studios was in Hollywood, too, Gary decided to help Walter fulfill his dream. Besides, Gary would never leave Walter behind!

Just the same, Gary promised to take Mary to a fancy dinner on the night of their anniversary. "It's gonna be the most romantic anniversary dinner ever!"

Mary couldn't wait.

WALTER was so EXCITED to see the studio where the Muppets used to perform. He secretly hoped that Kermit the Frog would be there!

But Gary didn't want Walter to get his hopes up. "The Muppets haven't put on a show together in years. I don't think they use the studios for anything but tours anymore."

Unfortunately, Gary was right. When the three friends got to the Muppet Studios, they saw that the theater looked broken down and dirty.

WALTER **was** DISAPPOINTED. He snuck into Kermit's old office, hoping to learn something about his hero.

"Now, this here is Kermit the Frog's old office."

Walter ducked and hid! He watched as Statler and Waldorf led a man named Tex Richman into the office. Tex said that he was going to buy the Muppet Studios and turn the place into a Muppet museum.

As SOON as Statler and Waldorf left, Tex revealed his real plan. "There's oil under this studio. In two weeks we tear this place to the ground and start drilling."

The only chance the Muppets had was to raise ten million dollars. That way, they could buy back their studio. Walter had to warn Kermit!

When WALTER, GARY, and MARY found Kermit, Walter was too nervous to get the words out. "Tex Richman, the . . . the oil baron . . . !" He almost fainted.

Kermit knew the only way to raise ten million dollars was to put on a show with the whole group. But the other Muppets had gone their separate ways.

KERMIT *found* FOZZIE BEAR performing in a stage show with the Moopets. They were kind of like the Muppets, only a lot meaner.

"We hired you, and we could fire you! So get in here now!"

"They terrify me. Let's go!" Fozzie couldn't wait to get away from the Moopets.

In his TIME AWAY from the MUPPETS, Gonzo had made a fortune selling toilets. But he was happy to leave the plumbing business behind and join up with Kermit again. Plus, he had missed performing his daredevil stunts.

"Citizens of Earth! The Great Gonzo is back! I pledge never to hold a plunger again!"

SOON, **they had found** ROWLF, ANIMAL, and the rest of the Muppets. They were all together again. Well, not all of them. Fozzie spoke up.

"Kermit, we're going to get Miss Piggy, right?"

MISS PIGGY *was in* PARIS, FRANCE. She worked for a fashion magazine there and had a very important position. The Muppets arrived at her office, and Kermit walked up to her desk.

"Hello, Piggy . . ."

Walter told her about how the studio was in danger.

BUT *she only* WANTED to speak with one person, er, frog. "Before I decide anything, I need to talk with you, Frog. *Moi et toi* . . . alone."

Kermit hadn't seen Miss Piggy in many years. They had had a big fight, and Piggy had left for France.

Piggy still loved Kermit, but she had her own life in Paris now.

KERMIT **had to** BREAK **it** to the rest of the Muppets that Miss Piggy was going to stay in Paris. Disappointed, they all went back to Hollywood, and Kermit hired Miss Poogy from the Moopets instead.

The MUPPETS began to visit television networks to see if anyone would broadcast their telethon show. They didn't have much luck.

"No."

"No."

"*Lo siento, perro no.*"

The Muppets didn't really understand.

"That means no."

FINALLY, a NETWORK decided to give them a shot—on one condition: they needed to get a celebrity host for the show. The Muppets happily went back to their old auditorium. But when they got there, they discovered that it was a mess!

Fozzie was doubtful. "Kermit, there's no way we can rehearse with the place like this!"

But GARY would not give up. "Mary, Walter, and I . . . well, we would be happy to help you rebuild the theater."

The Muppets had a great time cleaning up the old auditorium. Gary noticed that Walter was fitting right in with his new friends. It made Gary feel a little sad to see his brother spending so much time with the Muppets. When Gary went to find Walter so they could clean the balcony, Walter was already helping Fozzie.

The NEXT DAY, Miss Piggy arrived. "There's only one Miss Piggy and she is *moi*!" And with one karate chop, Piggy knocked out Miss Poogy.

The Muppets were happy to see Piggy again, but everything else was a disaster. The timing was off in the opening song, most of the acts were rusty, and Kermit couldn't find a celebrity host.

KERMIT *didn't* KNOW *what* TO DO. "I might as well just go and ask Tex Richman to give us the studio back. . . ." So that is just what the Muppets did.

But Tex wouldn't budge. "The world has moved on! Now get out of my office!" Tex hated the Muppets because he had never been able to laugh.

AS *if* THINGS couldn't get worse, Tex then revealed that he planned
to replace the Muppets with the Moopets! Kermit felt defeated. But
Piggy refused to let the oil baron tear down their theater. "All right,
listen up you freaks! I didn't come five thousand miles to *not* be on
TV." And she led the Muppets on a mission to find a celebrity host.

BACK at the THEATER, Walter was getting very excited about the telethon. Kermit had even asked him to perform! But Gary was feeling a little down. With each day, Walter was becoming closer to the Muppets . . . and less of a brother to Gary. And now Mary was mad at him.

"I'm going to go for a walk. Individually." She left to see the sights of Hollywood on her own.

SUDDENLY, GARY FIGURED OUT why Mary was angry at him. Today was their anniversary, and he had forgotten!

Mary left a note: "Gary, I've gone home. I love you, but you need to decide. Are you a man or a Muppet?"

Gary finally knew that the most important thing in his life was Mary, not the Muppets. He left for Smalltown to get her back.

MEANWHILE, PIGGY and a few of the other Muppets had somehow kidnapped a Hollywood actor to host their show!

When she told Kermit about it, he got hopping mad.

Fozzie argued that saving the Muppets was more important than breaking the law.

Kermit couldn't believe his ears. (Do frogs even have ears?)

At LAST, everything was ready for the show. They had sets. They had acts. They had costumes. They even had a celebrity host, even if he kept trying to escape.

The curtain was about to go up. There was just one problem: they didn't have an audience, which meant the producer from the TV network was not happy. "Where's the audience? I knew you guys weren't popular anymore!"

KERMIT **would not** let this get him down. "Scooter, did you hand out all those flyers?"

"Well of course, every last one."

Kermit made a decision. Audience or no audience, the Muppets were going to do what they did best: perform. He was sure that if they had the chance to make people laugh, the fans would show their support.

The SHOW BEGAN. It didn't go as smoothly as it had in the old days. Some of the songs were a bit off-key. Gonzo couldn't pull off his bowling-ball trick. (Literally, he couldn't pull the bowling ball off his fingers.) Their host was a *hostage*. But it was still a great show. People started watching it on their TVs. And soon, the auditorium was full. The Muppet telethon had an audience!

WHEN *it was* TIME for Walter's act, he panicked and ran offstage. He just wasn't ready to perform in front of all those people! The Muppets were about to go on with the show, but just then, Tex arrived. "Well, that's that. Nice try, Muppets!" He took an ax to the electrical wires for the building, and all the lights went out! Luckily, Mary and Gary had returned just in time, and Mary fixed the lighting.

DONATIONS were POURING in. The show was raising a lot of money! But the best news was that Kermit and Miss Piggy had finally patched things up. Kermit admitted to Piggy that he had missed her. "Maybe you don't need the whole world to love you. Maybe you just need one person."

The PERFORMANCES ONSTAGE were getting better and better. People all across the country called in to donate money. The Muppets were very close to their goal!

Walter knew that it was now or never. He walked onstage and finally did his act. He whistled beautifully, and the fans loved it.

By the TIME WALTER FINISHED his song, the Muppets had raised $9,999,999! They just needed one more dollar!

And that was when Tex knocked over a telephone pole outside, and the phones stopped ringing. The clock struck midnight, and it was all over. Tex had won, after all. "Game over, Kermit. You lost."

The MUPPETS *were* CRUSHED. But they knew this wasn't the end for them. Kermit encouraged his friends. "Let's just start at the bottom and work our way back up to the top! Let's all walk out through these doors with our heads held high. As a family."

And when they stepped out of the theater, a cheering crowd was waiting for them.

TEX **was** INFURIATED. Just then, Gonzo finally finished his bowling-ball trick. "Hey, guys, I think I've finally worked out how to . . . whaaa!"

The bowling ball flew off his hand and right into Tex's head!

FOZZIE **made a** PUN. "*Oil* bet that hurt." Tex laughed—for the first time in his life! He was so happy that he decided to give the Muppets back their studio. Of course, it had nothing to do with the fact that he had a head injury. . . .

Walter thought he couldn't be any happier. But then Kermit asked him to join the Muppets. And Gary asked Mary to marry him! Everything had a happy ending . . . even this book.